Tip Tap Sam

and

Not a Nut

'Tip Tap Sam' and 'Not a Nut'
An original concept by Jenny Moore
© Jenny Moore

Illustrated by Karl West

Published by MAVERICK ARTS PUBLISHING LTD

Studio 11, City Business Centre, 6 Brighton Road,

Horsham, West Sussex, RH13 5BB

© Maverick Arts Publishing Limited August 2021

+44 (0)1403 256941

A CIP catalogue record for this book is available at the British Library.

ISBN 978-1-84886-809-0

www.maverickbooks.co.uk

This book is rated as: Pink Band (Guided Reading)
It follows the requirements for Phase 2 phonics.
Most words are decodable, and any non-decodable words are familiar,
supported by the context and/or represented in the artwork.

Tip Tap Sam

and

Not a Nut

By
Jenny Moore

Illustrated by
Karl West

The Letter P

Trace the lower and upper case letter with a finger. Sound out the letter.

Down,
up,
around

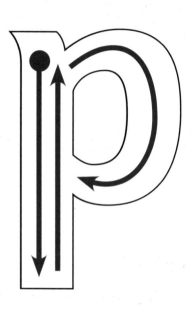

Down,
up,
around

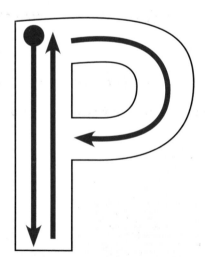

Some words to familiarise:

hat   cat   rug

High-frequency words:

I   on   the   in

Tips for Reading 'Tip Tap Sam'

- Practise the words listed above before reading the story.

- If the reader struggles with any of the other words, ask them to look for sounds they know in the word. Encourage them to sound out the words and help them read the words if necessary.

- After reading the story, ask the reader why Sam could not tap on the tap.

Fun Activity

Try tap dancing!

Tip Tap Sam

I can tap on the hat.

I can tap on the cat.

I can tap on the rug.

I can tap in the mug.

Can I tap on the tap?

I cannot!

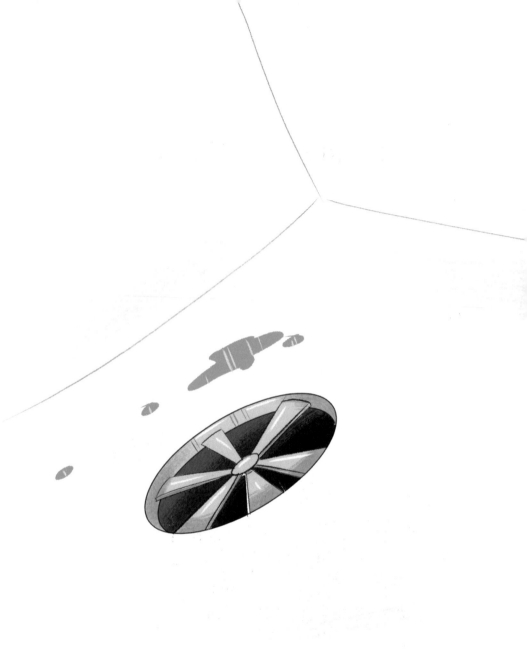

But I can tap in the tub!

The Letter O

Trace the lower and upper case letter with a finger. Sound out the letter.

Around

Around

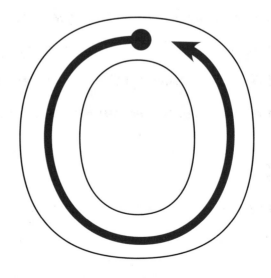

Some words to familiarise:

dig

hug

High-frequency words:

is   it   a

Tips for Reading 'Not a Nut'

- Practise the words listed above before reading the story.

- If the reader struggles with any of the other words, ask them to look for sounds they know in the word. Encourage them to sound out the words and help them read the words if necessary.

- After reading the story, ask the reader what the item was.

Fun Activity

Discuss what else you might find at a beach.

Not a Nut

Is it a hat?

It is not.

Is it a nut?

It is not.

Can it dig?

It cannot.

Can it cut?

It cannot.

Can it hug?

It cannot!

But it can run!

Book Bands for Guided Reading

The Institute of Education book banding system is a scale of colours that reflects the various levels of reading difficulty. The bands are assigned by taking into account the content, the language style, the layout and phonics. Word, phrase and sentence level work is also taken into consideration.

Maverick Early Readers are a bright, attractive range of books covering the pink to white bands. All of these books have been book banded for guided reading to the industry standard and edited by a leading educational consultant.

To view the whole Maverick Readers scheme, visit our website at www.maverickearlyreaders.com

Or scan the QR code above to view our scheme instantly!